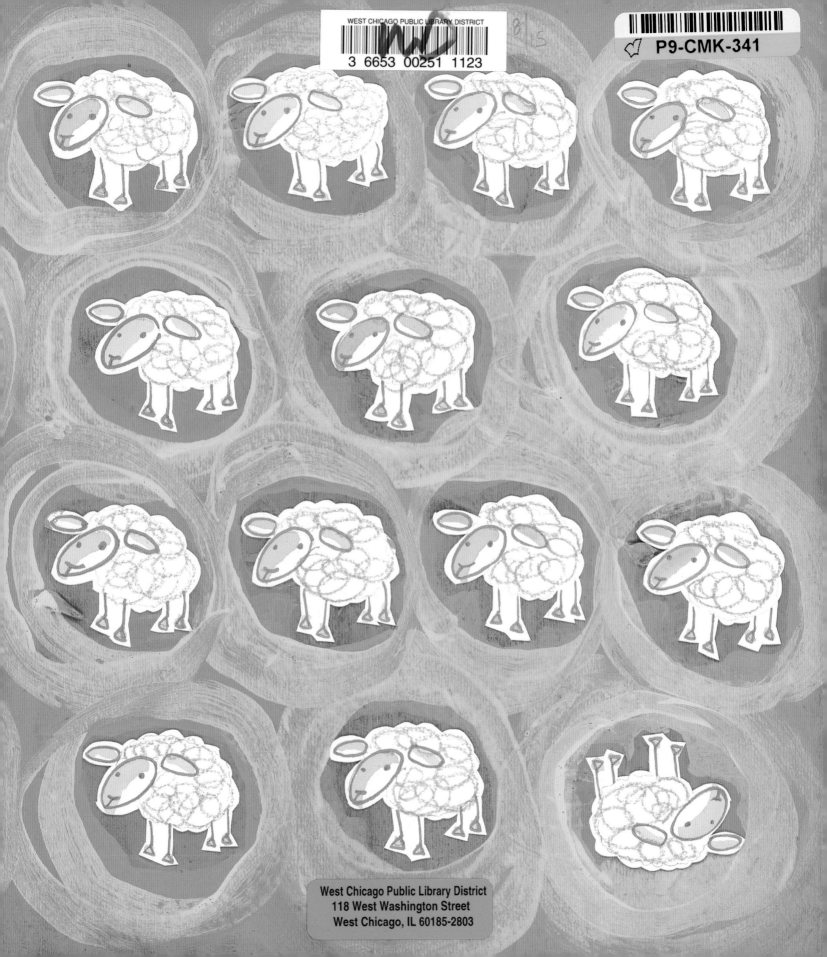

CRYBABY

To welcome your brand-new baby boy,
this book is dedicated to Leah, DG,
Lila, and Tyler, with love.
—K. B.

To Mary, Isaac, and Ezra
—E. Y.

Henry Holt and Company, LLC
Publishers since 1866
175 Fifth Avenue
New York, New York 10010
mackids.com

Henry Holt® is a registered trademark of Henry Holt and Company, LLC.
Text copyright © 2015 by Karen Beaumont
Illustrations copyright © 2015 by Eugene Yelchin
All rights reserved.

Library of Congress Cataloging-in-Publication Data
Beaumont, Karen.
Crybaby / Karen Beaumont : illustrated by Eugene Yelchin.—First edition.
pages   cm
Summary: When Baby cries, her family and neighbors try unsuccessfully to stop her tears and get
her back to sleep, but Roy, the old retriever, knows that Baby needs her toy sheep for a good night.
ISBN 978-0-8050-8974-5 (hardback)
[1. Babies—Fiction. 2. Crying—Fiction. 3. Dogs—Fiction. 4. Family life—Fiction. 5. Bedtime—Fiction.] I. Title.
PZ7.B3805795Cry 2015   [E]—dc23   2014036094

Henry Holt books may be purchased for business or promotional use. For information on bulk purchases, please contact the
Macmillan Corporate and Premium Sales Department at (800) 221-7945 x5442 or by e-mail at specialmarkets@macmillan.com.

First Edition—2015 / Designed by April Ward
Printed in China by Macmillan Production Asia Ltd., Kowloon Bay, Hong Kong (vendor code: 10)

1   3   5   7   9   10   8   6   4   2

CRYBABY

Karen Beaumont

Illustrated by
Eugene Yelchin

Henry Holt and Company

NEW YORK

In a quiet house
on a quiet street . . .

. . . a not-so-quiet baby cried . . .

W-A-A-A-A!

She woke Roy, the old retriever, when she cried.

In no time that big dog was by her side.

BARK!
BARK!

She woke her mother and
her father when she cried.

Father hurried
to the baby . . .
Rush, rush!

Mother tried to
quiet Baby . . .
Hush, hush!
Rush, rush!

But the more
they tried,
the more that
baby cried . . .

W-A-A-A-A!

No, Roy! Down, boy!
Baby doesn't want that toy.

W-A-A-A-A!

BARK! BARK!

No, Roy!

Down, boy!

Baby doesn't want that toy.

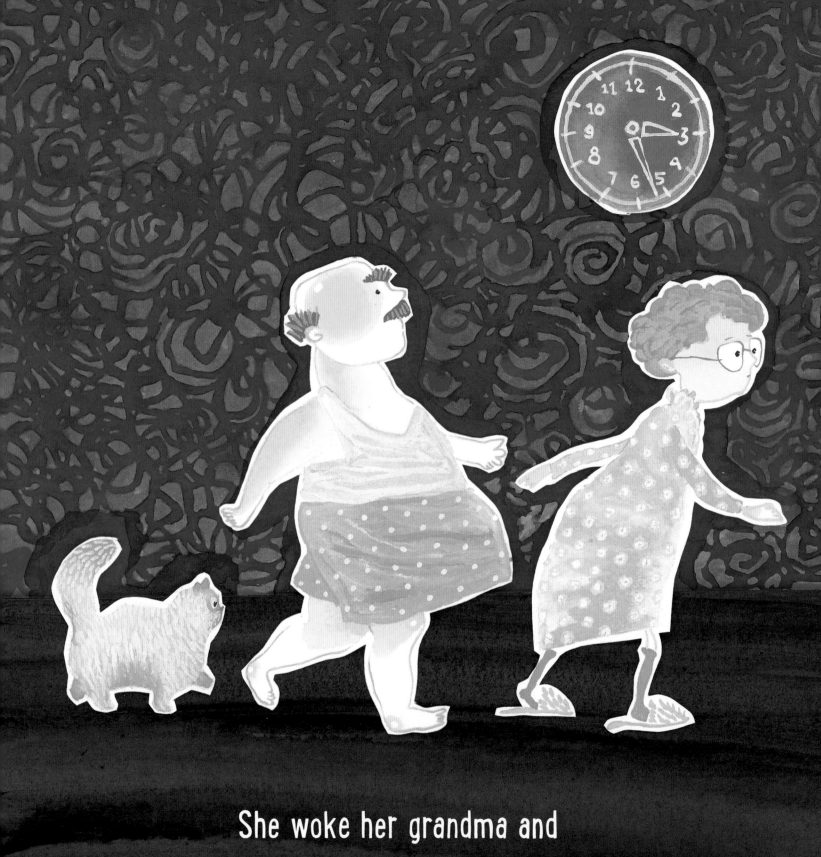

She woke her grandma and
her grandpa when she cried.

Grandma tried to feed the baby . . .

Slurp, slurp!

Grandpa tried to
burp the baby . . .

Burp, burp!
Slurp, slurp!
P-e-e-u-u-w-w!
Peek-a-boo!
Hush, hush!
Rush, rush!

But the more they tried, the more that baby cried . . .

W-A-A-A-A!

BARK! BARK!
No, Roy!
Down, boy!
Baby doesn't want that toy.

She woke the sleepy next-door neighbors when she cried.
They came in their pajamas . . . Knock, knock!

The neighbors
rocked the baby . . .
Rock, rock!
Knock, knock!

Burp, burp!
Slurp, slurp!
P-e-e-u-u-w-w!
Peek-a-boo!
Hush, hush!
Rush, rush!

But the more they tried, the more that baby cried . . .

W-A-A-A-A!

BARK! BARK!
No, Roy!
Down, boy!
Baby doesn't want that toy.

Still that old retriever
wouldn't leave her side.
No, Roy!
Down, boy!

Baby reaches for her toy,
a white and woolly little sheep.

Baby smiles,
then falls asleep.

Quiet Baby . . . what a joy!

Good boy, Roy!